Miscellaneous Madness

Jordana Kagan

Miscellaneous Madness by Jordana Kagan
Copyright © 2022 Jordana Kagan
Beats Books Barbells Press

Cover design by nskvsky.
Author portrait by Same Haze Graphics

Paperback ISBN: 979-8-9862545-1-7

Printed in the United States of America

This is mostly a work of fiction. Chapters are loosely
based on faulty recollections, fanciful ruminations, and
romances gone awry. I have changed some details to protect
the innocent.

Dad, I miss you every day.
It has not gotten easier.

Contents

A man put his life in my hands, and I let him die.

When I was twenty-two, I flew abroad to volunteer. The soup kitchen served mainly older men who had no one left to care about them.

I spoke the language, barely. Fluent enough to have simple conversations. But not enough to easily fulfill what he asked of me.

I don't remember his name—only that he claimed to have had an interesting life. He had been in the wars, he told me during our first encounter. He had seen things.

He returned the following day to give me his manuscript, a pile of mimeographed A3 papers, 11.69 by 16.53 inches. It was his life. He wanted me to tell it. I was American. People would listen.

I told him I couldn't read it. The language was too advanced. True.

Also true: I didn't want the responsibility. But I didn't tell him that.

It was important, he said. I needed to translate it and share it with the world.

Instead, I returned to the States and placed the story of this old man's life on my bookshelf next to my copy of *The Complete Works of William Shakespeare*. It rested there, peacefully, until seven years later. I was moving. Abroad. I packed some books and sold off others. I looked at his now-yellowed manuscript and remembered. Still unable to decipher the words, I chucked it in the paper receptacle.

A man placed his life in my hands, and I killed him.

I was young.

I didn't understand.

It haunts me.

And so, I write stories of those unseen and unheard.

An act of contrition.

A prayer for forgiveness.

Damian

Birthday Surprise

"It's wet."

"Mmm, hmm."

"It's like a…like a… It's slippery. It's like a slime!"

The little girl was mighty pleased with herself for getting this far. She normally couldn't contain her excitement long enough to keep her eyes closed. It was Hazel's birthday, and Damian was her best friend. He knew her best and always brought Hazel the most special gifts. To his credit, Damian sat motionless opposite her, save for the grin that widened with the girl's every guess. He didn't want to spoil the surprise, but he was ready to jump out of his pants. This was the best present the boy could *ever* think of. He was lucky he found it. And just in time.

Hazel, forcing her eyes closed, continued to probe inside the cardboard shoebox.

"It's soft. It's soft and slimy. It's a frog!" she squealed with delight as her eyes exploded open. "Damian, it's a frog!"

The boy laughed heartily. He could tell she liked it even more than the firefly he caught for her last summer.

Jordana Kagan

Departure

He stared ahead imagining the imprint she would have made had she been beside him, the weight of her form pressing against the durable dark-blue of the Long Island Rail Road seat.

They rode together every morning, he and Hazel, until her body could no longer contend with the commute. She was able to work remotely for a time, but then had to stop altogether; perhaps she'll return. *Maybe after the next one*, he thought.

Damian closed his eyes and smiled dreamily at the thought of his beloved wife, now working from home in a different capacity, cradling their newborn daughter, Rose.

False Hope

"You're right," he confirmed, looking at the scans.

"I had a feeling," she breathed in disbelief.

"Congratulations, Hazel." He smiled warmly. It had been a painful journey for both doctor and patient.

"Thank you." Tears of relief overcame her.

Misdiagnosis.

Underwear, Under Where?

It's cold and I have to pee. Actually, I have to shit. I didn't shit this morning. Fucking kids. It really isn't that hard. It's not like we haven't done it a million times before. Just put on your fucking underwear. Fucking underwear. *Because you wear it* under *your fucking clothes. Fucking... I can't with this shit.*

"Mommy?"

Sigh. "What is it, babe?"

"It's cold."

"I know, babe. Next time put your underwear on. Then Daddy can drive us, and we won't have to walk in the snow."

"Mommy?"

"Yes, Rosie?"

"I have to pee."

Jesus.

It was not yet 8:00, but Hazel was done for the day.

Preparation

"Fuck me."

No more than a whisper.

"Fuck me," she begged again, eyes dilating as she embraced the weight of his frame.

Farewell.

Jordana Kagan

Frozen Toes

The little girl shrieked.

Her father came running, one side of his face dripping from the interrupted shave.

"What's wrong? What happened?" Damian scanned the cabin for invisible threats, understanding danger often lurked undetected.

"My toes are cold!" Rosie informed him.

He looked at her, shaken and baffled. It was winter. In Burlington. They were going tobogganing.

"Daddy, your face is wet."

The grip of fear released him—for the moment. Damian could deal with the eight-year-old's frozen toes, but if anything should happen to Rose... He wouldn't be able to handle another catastrophe.

Connecting

Did she know how much he loved her? He was scared of saying the wrong thing, scared of losing her.

Rosie was a teenager now. Volatile. She relished riding the ups and downs, the self-discovery. She was unaware of how strangely, how uncannily, how unimaginably painfully and beautifully she resembled her mother, Hazel.

Hazel.

Jordana Kagan

In Another Life

I dream of you in my waking hours,
Sun-filled scenes of juicy, joyful love.

In the shadows of sunset,
My body inches closer,
My skin burning for you
As I touch the smooth coolness of the unforgiving wall.
I remember then,
And despair.

Choices

"No, weirdo. I told you I don't believe in marriage."

They had stopped at the end of the four-mile boardwalk to stretch, part of their nightly ritual.

He smiled sheepishly, grateful Rosie hadn't been facing the shore, that she hadn't seen his heart vulnerable in the sand.

Missed-demeanor.

Jordana Kagan

Unlimited

They told me yesterday.
I didn't have time to process.

I was on my way to a meeting.
I didn't want to cancel. We had already rescheduled it.
Twice.
I should have canceled—to save everyone time.
So they won't have to repeat themselves.
Since I won't be there. Moving forward.

It was a question of when, really.
Metastatic breast cancer running back three generations.
I'm the fourth—
I'm the last.

It was a deliberate decision, and not a difficult one, to not have kids.
Thirty-eight years.
All the perspective I need for my final three months.

"Rosie?" Damian's voice echoed from the kitchen and roused her. "You wanted to tell me something?"

"Coming, Dad." She capped the pen, closed the notebook, and felt the crushing weight of goodbye.

Alone

"It moves too fast... so fast, I didn't realize..."

Damian stood, feet planted in the soft, freshly cut grass, staring at the trees, listening to the birds, breathing spring.

"The other day, I forgot... I was calling you both from the living room... to see... There was a bluebird..."

He paused, reliving.

"Everything went by too fast."

He felt the warmth of the sun's rays on his face and the gentle breeze that tickled the hairs on his arms.

"It went by too fast," he choked.

Jordana Kagan

A Perfect Day

I wake,
Salt crusted in the corners of my eyes.
I must have been crying
In my sleep
Again.
Is it a blessing or a curse that I cannot recollect?
A bit of respite because I don't remember.
Breathless terror—
I might forget
Your face
Your voice
Your scent.
I can feel you—
Still—
If I close my eyes.

Betsy

Looking In

She was an invisible, like me. A tiny girl sitting ramrod straight, hands in her lap, face staring ahead. He sat on her right, leaning in. Hovering. His left arm wrapped around her from behind. His right arm around her front closed the cage.

His hands were huge.

He was familiar with her.

Her eyes were darting from side to side, but her head was still. I looked for any suggestion of comfort in her posture and found none.

It was 10:47 p.m. on the E train. I left her there, with him, when we got to Jackson Avenue. We were not seen. Not me. Not her.

That's What Friends Are For

Oblivious. That's what her parents thought. Actually, it was willful ignorance. Betsy's coping mechanism. The only way she knew how to deal with the truth of her reality was by not admitting it existed. She *couldn't* see it. If she did, her world would crumble.

So, Betsy colored. With her eight best friends: Black, Brown, Red, Orange, Yellow, Green, Blue, and Purple. They were, in fact, her only friends. The ones who held her trusted secrets. In confidence. In faith. Because they saw. Through her drawings, the crayons gave witness.

"Maybe we should do something," Green suggested, as he lay waiting for his turn. Today he would fill in the grass, but first Betsy had to finish with Yellow; she was making a flower.

"Our influence over the current circumstances is limited, you know." Black, the realist of the group, didn't mean to be dismissive. In truth, he felt more connected to Betsy than the others. She always drew with him first. Black was the color she used to shape her sorrows. The privilege pained him.

"No, no. I think Green is on to somethin'."

"Ah, Red, you always get excited about stuff. As much as I hate to admit it, Black is right. We're stuck." This was a difficult admission for Blue. Betsy always relied on him for hope, to color the skies of a brighter day.

"You never know," Purple offered. "I mean, with all that's been happening. I don't know. I mean, shouldn't we at least try?"

"Try what, Purple?"

"Try to help, Orange. I mean, I don't know. Like, for Betsy. We should try to help."

"Yeah, okay. But how? You got any suggestions? You got a plan?"

"Easy, Brown. Purple, do you have a plan?" Blue asked, feeling hopeful.

"I have a plan, guys!" Yellow interrupted. She was back on the table as Betsy swapped her for Green. "Oh, boy, do I have a plan."

That night, after the house had quieted, they all agreed. Yellow's plan was fantastic, but they had to time it perfectly. They *had* to. For Betsy.

The next morning, they stood like soldiers, waiting for their most important mission. Ms. Marie invited all the children to the coloring station. Betsy followed her classmates. Slowly. Tentatively. It had been a rough night. She hesitated before opening the box and greeting her friends. She smiled when she saw their colorful stubs. Black. Brown. Red. Orange. Yellow. Green. Blue. Purple. Betsy didn't know this would be their last picture together.

Black began, as was his custom, outlining. Carefully. Precisely. Red rolled into Betsy's hand before the child had a chance to think what to do next. Green inched closer. Betsy grabbed him. Blue knew what to do. Orange. Brown. Purple. Yellow. Each color guiding her fingers until the picture was complete. Each one vigilant, lest Ms. Marie see the drawing before the story was finished.

But now, it was.

Betsy looked up, her eyes wet.

Ms. Marie approached, kneeling with concern.

Arms outstretched, Betsy displayed her picture. Her friends rolled aside, toward one another.

Ms. Marie's face froze. She blinked. She looked at Betsy and knew it was true.

Collage

Betsy inspected her fingers: sticky, speckled with glitter, stained with dye, crusted with acrylic.

She had decorated the room with a hodgepodge of collages, pictures she had pasted together herself. A mosaic of color that would celebrate her first decade. Snapshots of memories she was too old to remember. Images of events she was too young to forget.

Jordana Kagan

Therapy

Again the girl sliced and was calmed by the warm blood bubbling up through the reopened the wound.

   She breathed.

   Relief.

Whispering

Sibilant whisperings reach my consciousness
But do not penetrate,
Too faint.
I strain against the weight of my skin.
My body is my prison.
My mind, my captor—
Refusing to release me from this life.

Peace awaits beyond—
I'm certain.
I hear it whispering.
I yearn to join its chorus.

Betsy Finds a Boy

"It's still raining."

"So, what do you want to do?"

"Come over. We'll drink tea and play Boggle."

Betsy was disappointed they wouldn't be able to go to the beach, but "third time's a charm," as they say. She had no doubt she would enjoy a low-key third date. She threw on her favorite basketball shorts and made the bed. The boy arrived shortly after. He was dressed to impress. *Odd*. It was only three o'clock and they had planned to stay in. She suddenly had the distinct impression that he would be meeting another girl after he skated out of her apartment. But Betsy didn't have time to dwell on that. She was about to pass out from his cologne. *Or is it aftershave? Or maybe it's chloroform? That's why guys do that! So they don't look like suspects after their date disappears and is found raped and murdered four months later—Stop catastrophizing*, she chided herself and opened the door wider for him to enter.

Betsy took his umbrella and made some tea. He preferred mint, not mango. *Even though there's only one mint left*! she noted. Betsy arranged the teacups, timer, and pens on the table, then made herself comfortable on the couch. When he didn't follow, she looked up, curious, and cocked her head sideways. He was standing in front of her, unbuttoning his shirt.

Um. Betsy was stunned.

His hand caressed his freshly shaven chest and down his stomach.

"Do you like my body?"

She liked his belt, but that was about it. He presented himself surprisingly well in clothes, considering what he was working with. *That's why he needed to knock me out with chloroform!* She smirked at her own joke, which he took as an affirmative. He seized her hands, kissing each one in turn, then lifted her up. His dad bod was deceitfully strong, but still no more appealing than before. She played along, wondering if this was how the scripts for bad pornos were contrived. But then she soured. *He wasted my last mint tea! Dick.* She completed this thought as he carried her to the bedroom.

She was still clothed, but he was down to boxers. *When did that happen?* She reciprocated by removing her shirt, and he attacked her bra with his mouth, slobbering all over it. Betsy should have been scared. She had been traumatized, after all, but had been making solid progress in therapy and was proud of herself. *This is too weird to be scary*, she decided as she stared up at the ceiling.

That's when the man-boy reversed his positioning—feet now at her head—and commenced running his tongue up and down her shins. *What the hell?* Betsy was immobilized. *He's humping my hip. Oh, my God. What the hell?* she thought as he suddenly paused and reared up. His pale, hairless ass was poised in the air. *When did he lose his boxers? What the hell?!*

27

Betsy was beginning to feel uncomfortable. And then it happened. His starry anus puckered and blew a kiss of death.

"Oh, my God." Betsy gasped and buried her face in the pillow to escape the smell of his fatal flatulence. He began licking her leg again, and she started to shake. With laughter, into the pillow lest she offend him. Betsy was still working on that in therapy. *I really shouldn't care so much about other people's feelings*, she reminded herself. She lifted her head to breathe, delirious with giggles and crying at the absurdity, when one of her tears fell on his ankle. That jolted him, and he bolted upright.

"Are you okay?" he asked, full of concern.

Betsy closed her eyes to center herself, but a few more tears squeezed out in the process. He smothered her in a hug; his eau de chloroform overpowered her. She couldn't speak.

"Tell me what's in your heart," he coaxed.

"I. Can't. Do. This," Betsy said, careful to stifle the laughter that was readying to gush forth.

He propped himself on one elbow, looked at her, his face gravely serious. "What did I do?"

Betsy could only shake her head vigorously in response, which seemed to cause more tears to spurt forth.

He gently wiped a droplet from the corner of her eye and brushed stray hairs away from her forehead.

She still couldn't look at him, fighting with all her might not to laugh at this poor fellow who was clearly worse off than she——*His penis is on my blanket!* She jumped up.

"I need you to leave. Now. I need you to leave," she insisted as she gathered his trail of clothes. In the process, she glimpsed her last mint tea cooling in the glass that his lips had not touched, and she seethed. *This is what my therapist keeps talking about*, she realized.

Jordana Kagan

A New Me

A crash woke her. Betsy's feet dragged her into the kitchen. The pot of Bolognese sauce was splattered on the tiles. A crow was standing on the dinner plate eating the other half of her baguette. The window was open. The autumn air chilled her as she stood in her boyfriend's T-shirt. *EX-boyfriend*, she pointedly recalled, watching dawn break.

I don't feel like crying, she thought while surveying the damage of her previous night's revelries.

"Are you an omen?" she wondered aloud. The crow brazenly ignored her and continued to feast.

She stared at its silhouette, slowly allowing everything to register.

The crow paused, bristled, and hopped past the wine glass to pick at what looked like a tasty morsel.

She removed her T-shirt.

He was unimpressed.

She shivered.

He flew out the open window.

Finally free, Betsy laughed.

Margaret

Little Games

"No."

　"Please?"

　"No."

　"After dinner?"

　"After dinner."

　The girl smiled.

　"Only one cookie and *only* if you finish eating dinner," the mother emphasized.

　Triumph.

Jordana Kagan

Two Are Better Than One

Dear Sally,
Guess what I did! But you already know. Mommy's gonna be so mad.

September 18, 1987

Dear Mrs. Andersen,

Thank you for sharing your concerns regarding your daughter, Margaret. I understand from your letters that you are distressed by her behavior, but please be assured: often, an only child will invent an imaginary friend. Margaret's behavior is quite normal, I am certain.

All the best,

Dr. Patrick King

Dear Sally,
How could you make Mommy cry like that? You're a very bad girl.

October 3, 1987

Dear Mrs. Andersen,

    What you described in your last letter was quite curious. I'd like to know more. It would be best to bring Margaret in for testing next week.

                         Kind regards,

                         Dr. Patrick King

Dear Sally,
You shouldn't have cut that girl's hair without permission. That was mean.

October 10, 1987
Mrs. Andersen,

It is imperative that we speak. The situation is urgent.

Dr. King

Dear Sally,

They're taking me away. They said that it's a special place, and there will be more kids like me to play with. I don't care how many kids there are. I want us to stay here with Mommy. *You* spoiled it! Why did you have to kill the cat? Now they think we're bad, and they're sending us away.

Self-Doubt

They don't want to engage.
Maybe I'm too much of a loose cannon.
Maybe they're scared.
They don't know which version of me is showing up.

Maybe it's not them.
Maybe it's me.

Jordana Kagan

Jekyll and Hyde

She laughs maniacally. It's happening again. Another wave of lucid epiphanies. Another chance for the world to make sense. Another week of connecting to everyone and everything. She screams, forcing herself forward with frenzied and frenetic urgency because there is so much to do and it's so important and why doesn't anyone else understand because it makes so much *sense*!

Until it doesn't.

She slumps. Deflated and defeated. An exhausted, bewildered shell. How did it slip so far beyond her grasp? Where did it go? It made so much sense. Everything. And now it's gone.

In her torpor, she can't be bothered to care. She has other, more primal concerns. Because it hurts. From the depths. And the remedy is not within reach. She roars in pain, and bathed in tears, she prays to forget.

Adaptation

I used to wait. Wait for days to be over. Wait for nights to end. Now, there's too much to do. I don't have time to wait. Maybe that's why... I would be suicidal if only I had a minute to stop and think. I'd think, *I'd like to not be here.*

Jordana Kagan

Coping

"No." The smell reached her from two flights down.

"No. No, no, no, no," she pleaded, as she fumbled with the keys in her quaking hands.

The super hadn't lied. In the wake of a citywide blackout, in the height of August's heat, the water filter had not restarted. Q-Bert and Fancy Pants, her two magnificent cuttlefish, were dead.

Sorrow.

Restless Spring

The waves are angry today.
That's what I thought as I watched them fight,
Wrestling so violently—
Until they foamed white.

Grabbing
And clinging
For as long as they could,
Until the sands and the winds ripped them apart.

Rushing at each other,
This time with greater force,
Begging, desperate pleas,
"Please, don't let go."

Jordana Kagan

A Bright Future

The future is still fresh,
Not yet tainted by my disappointing touch,
Not yet betrayed by my duplicity,
Not yet ruined—by me.

The future holds hope,
Of what I might achieve,
Of what I might build,
Of what I might see.

The future brings pain,
In the unfulfillment of today,
In the knowledge of failure,
A failure without lesson,
Without change,
A failure that will be
Without escape,
Without reprieve.

Amnesia

He smiled at the sculpture. "My wife made that," he said to the college student standing next to him.

Henry, who was an art major, was notably impressed. He didn't need to look at the plaque. Margaret Sigmore-Andersen was as famous for her art as she was for her death, a gruesome and untimely event that the entire world had mourned. Six years ago.

"She teaches at Pratt, these days," the gentleman continued. "But we're thinking of leaving the city for Europe." He winked in confidence.

The young man looked at the elder with a sudden echo of recognition. When it had happened, Henry had still been a teenager, hadn't yet dealt with his own personal tragedies.

"Barry?" Henry was astonished.

Barry, the elder, beamed. He wasn't used to being recognized. It was his wife who drew the attention and accolades.

"You're—" The young man stopped himself.

"Have you met my wife, Margaret?"

"No, sir." *It's true*, he marveled. *The old man really doesn't remember.*

"Well, stick around. She finishes at three and we always grab a quick bite before she heads to the studio."

Barry

Boys Will Be Boys

"Hubba Bubbalicious." The boy grinned. Sheltered from the summer sun in the shadow of the tree, his mouth worked into a knot as his trembling fingers pried at the once-white wrapping. Red letters melded into pink patches where his salty sweat mingled with the gooey watermelon gum. The formerly crisp cube was now a squashed, sticky pancake— the result of one long hour running and falling, playing stickball and tag. The boy stood and unwrapped his treasure.

"You're it!" Caleb jolted him and ran off.

The pink blob of magical goodness flopped to the dirt. The boy looked at it—hesitating long enough to evaluate the gravity of the situation. Then, in one graceful swipe, he lifted the gum to his mouth and sprinted after his friend.

Jordana Kagan

Lovebirds

"I'm excited."

"Me too."

The lovebirds looked at one another, heads cocked sideways. "Are you sure you want to do this?"

Emmi paused. Her talons gripped the edge of the cactus.

"I'm ready. Ready to do it," she affirmed.

Ife quivered and ruffled his colorful breast feathers to mask a hint of trepidation. Humans had been the ones to catch and cage them, after all. They were taking a risk by exposing themselves. It had only been two weeks since Emmi and Ife had escaped the aviary. Since then, the exotic birds had been surviving on scant scraps of grass and residing in cacti as they made their way through the perilous desert.

Yesterday they arrived in Phoenix and were welcomed by the enticing sight of colorful bird feeders and the hum of air-conditioning.

It was time to embark on a new phase in their adventure. They were ready to begin again. Together.

Barry Learns the Hard Way

Candace heard a sound. A dull thud against the pane of the front door.

Strange, she thought.

The thud beckoned her again.

"Coming!" she called, with a note of unsurety.

Candace looked through the glass. Nothing. She opened the door and was met by a blast of Phoenix heat. All was quiet.

I wonder what——she couldn't finish her thought. The sight of two beautiful lovebirds lying——*stunned or dead?*——on the front stoop paralyzed her.

"Oh, my!" she gasped. "Barry! Barry!"

"What is it, Mom? What's wrong?"

"Come quick. Bring a shoe box and a towel!"

Jordana Kagan

Valiant Effort

"No." The director made a note and shuffled her papers. "Next."

"No? But—are you sure?" the comedian pressed.

"Yeah, kid. You're not funny. Come back when you have some new material. No more knock-knock jokes."

Rejection.

Not Forgotten

"Barry?"

He hated this conversation. Hated that she always circled back to it.

"Don't you love me?"

"C'mon. Don't do that."

"If you loved me—"

"Stop."

"*No*! If you loved me, you'd—"

"*Stop*! Goddammit. Margaret, I love you. With all my being, I love you."

"Then kill me." She searched his face. "Please." The silence hung in the air. "Before it's too late." There was no hope here. "Before..." She composed herself. "You know what will happen to me if you don't."

He knew. It had been hard, all these years. But she was getting better, wasn't she?

Jordana Kagan

Paper, Not Plastic

They do not stop.
They do not stop for me.
They do not stop even when their eyes rest upon me.

I beg.
I plead in silence.
But no.
They will not see me.

Before, they would.
At least to show
Sadness
Regret
Disgust.
At least they saw—something.
Occasional change.
A dollar bill.
I could buy coffee.
Something soft to stave off the hunger.

Now no one carries change.
And I cannot see my reflection when they stare through me.

Hannah

In the Bedroom

I can't hear what they're saying, but it doesn't really matter. I snuck up to my bedroom when they started yelling at each other and hid in the closet with Rusty. But Daddy knows all my hiding spots and he can always find me easy.

I need to be able to see my bedroom doorknob because as long as I'm using all my powers to keep it locked then I'll be safe, but it's really hard because when I blink I lose all my powers and that's when Daddy comes in. So I'm working really hard to not blink and Rusty is trying to help but he doesn't have special powers like me because he's only a stuffed rockwilder.

The pins and needles in my arm really hurt but I have to concentrate on keeping the door locked so I can't move yet.

Last time Daddy came in when I was already sleeping, and I woke up when he sat on my bed. He told me not to be scared because him and Mommy were only pretend fighting and he would never want me to be hurt or afraid. But I'm not stupid, I know he was lying. He pulled my blankets off and started rubbing my back. But I didn't want him to and I started crying just like I'm crying now.

I wish Rusty could cry instead of me because I just had to blink to get the wet out of my eyes and now daddy is standing in the doorway.

Relapse

I didn't know it was going to be like this. I don't want to give up, not after everything everyone did for me, but I'm not sure I can do it. I would rather be doing something else. Something... But it won't make me feel better. At least, not when I wake up tomorrow. If I wake up... I have to remember what they told me at the Center.

"You can't give up on something until you've actually tried."

"Stick with the process; you'll reach the outcome."

"Be the person who has something to contribute."

But what do I have to contribute? God! I wish I could be the girl that people turned to for help. I want to be a role model that they can look up to. One they can be proud of. I just... I want to be proud of *myself*. I wish... But, why not? I can do hard things. I can fix problems and get stuff done. And if I ask Rose, she can help me stick with it. I *can* do this. I don't have to keep living in the past. I can make new choices. I can make things better.

Boys Suck

Hannah poked her head out of the classroom door, practically resting her chin on her tiny teacher's head. The girl scanned the crowded hallway while the teacher encouraged the dawdlers to make haste and get to their classes.

"Where are they?" the girl wondered aloud before consulting the time on her phone.

"Who are you looking for?" the teacher asked.

Hannah shrugged. She had a round face and seemed young for her age, despite her tall frame. The girl was one of the top students in her class—on paper. But she was heartbreakingly shy and withdrawn.

The late bell rang.

"I hate boys," the girl said.

"Me too," the teacher agreed.

The girl looked at the diminutive woman.

"Why?" The girl needed to know—she was hesitant with hope, unable to hide her dimples.

"Because sometimes boys distract us from what's really important."

"Yeah," the girl said after a pause. "That's actually true."

The teacher smiled at the girl who, seemingly an inch taller, turned and walked to her seat.

Jordana Kagan

Bad Habits

"Again?!" She sweated, raw from the pain.

"I want another angle." He leered, one hand on the camera, the other maintaining his erection.

"But——" she attempted in vain.

"C'mon, ass up. You knew what you were signing up for."

Despair.

August in New York

The doors open and the fetid, sour stench of bodies hits, throwing me off balance. No choice. I have to get into the car. My eyes capture...

Three men in work boots. *Safe.*

Two women huddled and speaking in hushed whispers. *Safe.*

One man sleeping on the far bench. One puddle of urine. One opened bag of McDonald's, partially digested food resting beside it. *Possible threat.* Hopefully, he won't wake up.

One couple, sleeping on opposite benches. Suitcases stowed next to them, handles tied to their wrists. They are scared. *Safe.*

One woman in a wheelchair draped in plastic bags—

The man on the far bench falls to the floor. Groans. Rolls into the food. Begins eating. He is lying in the urine. I have two more stops to go. Where is God?

Jordana Kagan

Doorbells

Bolt awake.
Time: 9:51.
Danger.
Heart hammers.
Adrenaline surges.
Don't breathe.
Fear.
Wait.
Listen.
Nothing.
Strain to see the sounds in the hallway.
Nothing.
Alone here.
Dark.
Keep the lights off.
Get to the door.
Barefoot.
Silent.
Door slams.
Another apartment?
Or someone hiding in the stairwell?
Slide the cover off the peephole.
Peek.
Nothing.
Whoever was outside is no longer outside.

Not that I can see.
Waiting for me to open the door?
Maybe it's the water filter?
No.
Not this late at night.
Should I call the super?
Time: 9:53.
Eternity.

Jordana Kagan

Hypocrisy

They do not "see" her. They are busy protesting against the injustices. They share posts and like videos and "educate" the uninformed.

Kony.

Palestine.

Afghanistan.

Ukraine.

"Don't you know?" they condescend, claiming their noise makes a difference. Amid their clamor she disappears.

They stand tall. Confident and posturing, they steal the spotlight for their own self-aggrandizement. They are not concerned with the truth. They cannot be bothered with her.

Because of them, she is invisible.

Second Chances

Hi, this is Hannah. Leave a message.

"Hey, Hannah. It's me, Rose. Sorry I missed you yesterday. I was working at the Center until late. I'm home today. Call me."

Hi, this is Hannah. Leave a message.

"Hannah? Is everything okay?"

Hi, this is Hannah. Leave a message.

"Hannah, call me back, please. It's Rose."

Hi, this is Hannah. Leave a message.

"Hannah! Where are you?!"

Hi, this is Hannah. Leave a message.

Sammy

The Struggle

"Time remaining, fourteen minutes."

    He raised his hand. She approached his desk.

    "Miss, what happens if we don't finish?"

    "Do the best you can."

    "I still have three pages left."

    "You have fourteen minutes. Do the best you can."

    Panic.

Go, Cart. Go!

"Go-Go-Go Cart? Hey, Dad," Sammy puffed, "what's this?"

Steven looked at his son—more than husky, horn-rimmed glasses, asthma made worse by the dusty, mildewy attic. *He's exactly like me*, Steven mused, feeling an unremitting sting as he glimpsed at what he must have looked like through everyone else's eyes at that age.

"Bet you didn't know your dad was an athlete," Steven winked.

"Aw, Dad, cut it out." Sammy was used to hearing what his mother had termed "Dad's tall tales."

"Bring it here, Sammy. I'll show ya."

Sammy wiped his nose on his sleeve and sniffed again as he whisked up more dust lumbering toward his father.

Steven took the magazine and held it with both hands. He had nearly forgotten, but there it was. His small portrait inlaid on the front page. It had been a while, but he recognized it: the chubby, dimpled cheeks; the close-lipped smile; the thick, black frames.

"Sammy?" He pointed at the picture. The boy followed the finger.

Hmmm, the boy thought. "Oh!" He looked at his father, who smiled in confirmation. The glasses were different, but no doubt about it. That was Sammy's dad on the cover of a magazine!

"When I was a little older than you, Sammy, I was a racing champion."

The boy turned the pages and found the article. It wasn't a tall tale! His dad was a winner. And that meant Sammy could be too.

Jordana Kagan

Treasure Hunt

Two brown-haired boys took turns guarding one another as they made their way down the path. One wrong move, one foolhardy step, would trigger the booby traps and leave them for dead—or so they imagined. They continued to scout and reconnoiter the area, collecting leaves for camouflage and stones for slingshots, slowly making their way around the house, dodging danger, searching for the buried treasure. They reasoned that this side of the house was more likely to lead to the hidden riches. The area was greener, and green symbolized money.

"They definitely hid it under the bushes."

"Or maybe under the roots of the apple tree."

"Yeah. That's the perfect place for it."

Ferociously determined, the friends took a shortcut past the patio and back to the fort where they could safely consult the map and strategize. There was only an hour left before sunset, before their mothers would call them to dinner. They had to hurry.

A Turn of Events

"Fuck me," he uttered.

    Distracted and jaded, I volleyed tepidly, "It worked?"

    Silence.

    I turned to look. "Fuck me."

    Vindication.

Jordana Kagan

Dream Girl

"Your right?" he asked, confused.

   "No, your right. My left." She smiled quietly to herself.
   "Oh, I see it. I see you!"
   Excitement.

A Wife and Her Husband

"Knock, knock."

"Yes, dear?"

"No, you're supposed to say, 'Who's there?'"

"But I know who's there. You're there."

"No. It's a joke."

"Oh."

"Knock, knock."

"This is the joke, right?"

"Yes. Jeez."

"And I'm supposed to say, 'Who's there?'"

"Yes."

"Okay."

"Ready?"

"Yes, dear."

"Knock, knock."

"Is it a funny joke?"

"Oh, my God!"

"Well, I want to know if I should expect to laugh or if I'm going to have to fake it."

"I can't with you sometimes."

"I know, dear. That's why I have to fake it—sometimes."

"What the—when? When did you fake it?"

"Well, last Saturday, for example. You seemed so proud of yourself for losing two pounds, as if your new body was enough to inspire an orgasm. It was certainly endearing, but not enough to orgasm."

"Wait, what? What the—You faked that? How did you...? How often do you...?"

"Knock, knock, dear. Knock, knock."

Countdown Begins

"How many?"

"Eighty-three, sir."

"Sammy, what am I supposed to do without a custodian for eighty-three days?"

"That's not something I considered, sir. But the rules say that if I don't take my unpaid sick leave before I retire, then I'll lose it completely."

"I can't pay you if you're not going to be here. I need a custodian for the school."

"You're not paying me, sir. The city pays me."

"The city can't pay a second custodian if one is already on the books."

"I didn't make the rules, sir."

"Eighty-three days?"

"With all the other holidays and whatnot, it'll be after Presidents' Week."

"You calculated?"

"I did."

"I'll be running a school for six months without a custodian? Jesus." The principal looked at Sammy, the man with the plan and the power. "Well, Sammy, congratulations. It's been a pleasure." The two men stood and shook hands. Firm and hearty. It had been seventeen years—the respect was mutual. "Now get out of here. I have phone calls to make to sort out this mess."

Angela

Be Aggressive

"Be aggressive. B-E aggressive. B-E-A-G-G-R-E-S-S-I-V-E. Be. Aggressive. B-E aggressive! Wooo!" Angela jumped and skipped and waved her pillowcases with enthusiasm. Rocky, Boo Boo Bear, and the rest of her dolls looked on as the aspiring cheerleader took her bow. For an encore, the little girl demonstrated the splits—at least as far as she could do in the splits. Angela added this move to her list of "Skills to Work On." She wasn't the most athletic. Usually, her asthma stopped her midroutine, and her glasses would always fly off during cartwheels. But today, cheeks flushed with pride, she did it! The whole cheer and the encore: 180 grueling seconds of burning passion. Angela was ready. She was going to shine like a star at the Midwood Middle School cheer tryouts.

Just Getting Started

"Again?" she asked officially, though they all already knew the answer.

"Again. Again." He waved in frustration. "We practice until we get it right."

The encroaching darkness would not deter them.

Perseverance.

See Something, Say Something

Angela blinked at me through thick lenses. "The numbers don't make sense," she insisted.

Angela. My new employee. Still green. Still under the impression she was hired to run numbers. She hadn't gotten the hang of it yet. Too bad Sabrina was gone. *Sabrina* knew what she was here for.

"Angela—"

"If you see something, say something. Right?"

She's serious.

"Well, I see something."

This poor girl fell in way over her head.

Jordana Kagan

Possibilities

Angela knew it was going to be a good day when her left eyelid started twitching. For some reason, her body could sense possibilities before she was aware they existed. Angela mindlessly executed her morning routine. It was rote by now, so she was free to focus on other things: usually work, sometimes love. Today she wondered what was on the road ahead. So many things could go right.

Young Love

"Again and again and again!" She danced while she dressed.

"You're a terrible singer," her lover noted.

"What should I dooo...?" She continued to belt off-key. Unfazed. He found her charming, she knew.

He chucked a pillow.

She dodged and wiggled her derriere.

Confidence.

Get It All Out

She curls over the toilet. Bile rising in a wave of pain, she vomits. Spits. Heaves some more. Unidentifiable pieces of her last meal splashing back in the fetid bowl.

"Oh, my God, what did I eat?" she pants.

Another heave. She braces herself.

"Uch. That smells so bad. Jeez."

She reaches to flush the toilet and is overcome by the smell of her own filth.

"Ugh."

She can't repress the reflex. Her stomach clenches again. The muscles and juices working against themselves to torture her.

"Ow. Fuck. Oh, my God."

Her heart begins to race. She's flushed and shivering.

"Owowow."

Another hurl. Clawing. Writhing. Excruciating.

"Pheeeeeeew."

She exhales deeply, choking once more on the acrid breath that clings to her nose and throat. She spits what's left from her mouth. Her throat is raw. Her nose is moist. She is exhausted from the exertion. Her stomach is empty. That, at least, brings a sense of relief. She opens her eyes.

"Oh, my God, it's the mango. I'm never eating mango again."

The Big Leap

The books were stacked, just not neatly. Dust bunnies stirred as she hefted the satchel resting in the corner. Keys. Wallet. Phone. All contained.

For weeks she grappled with the decision, avoided making one.

"Unable to," she comforted herself.

"Unnecessary," Sammy had said—he didn't empathize with her dilemma.

She finally announced her intentions this morning, in his absence—for Angela is converting to vegetarianism today, and Sammy will have to make do with soy burgers from now on.

Jordana Kagan

Musk

I smell danger. It is his musk. It attacks, reminding me that
he is a man, a man who hasn't showered today or yesterday.
The scent clings to the hairs of his armpit. His skin absorbs
the odor, which spreads and assaults my eyes and nose when
he smothers me during sex. Both the smell and the
suffocation arouse me. I can't hold back and race toward the
orgasm, but he won't allow it. He's not ready. He's enjoying
me, using me—the way a man should. I crave the release,
urging him deeper as I bury my face into his man-smell and
gasp for want of oxygen.

He likes this game, likes giving me what I want. He grabs
my thighs and opens me, easing deeper inside. I shudder with
pleasure and feel the contractions as I start fighting back. I
need space. I need air. He holds me down until he finishes.
Then, still panting, I realize how badly he stinks, and tell him
so.

Grace

We Are Family

"Again!" The girls squeaked in unison.

Unable to refuse the pearls of his heart, the burly father sucked helium from the pink balloon and sang "Happy Birthday."

His twin daughters laughed breathlessly, overcome with glee.

Love.

Networking

"Golly! That looks great, Grace."

"Thanks! I thought if I mixed the purple with the green, it might make the netting look like an ocean, but it didn't turn out that way."

"No, I think blue and green go better for the ocean. But I like the way yours is coming out. Will you teach me how you do the crossover stitch?"

"Sure!"

Sabrina sat next to her sister. Together they worked— two bony, knock-kneed girls covered in freckled sunburns, mosquito bites, and crusty pink calamine lotion—weaving the story of their summer into the threads of Camp Hakaluugui's memory quilt.

Home Alone

"You're out of your mind."

She stayed silent.

"What the fuck, Sadie?"

She waited. Staring openly at him.

"We're not robbing a fucking bank."

"The plan is perfect."

"Perfectly insane. Perfectly stupid. Perfectly—"

"Lower your voice."

He glared at her.

"We won't get caught."

"We won't get caught because we aren't doing it." He stood and stomped to the door, readying to leave.

"Wait!" She slinked over to him. Grabbing the waist of his jeans. "What can I do to change your mind?"

"It's too big of a risk."

"Too big...?" she whispered knowingly, feeling him harden as she pressed in closer.

Smiling, he grabbed her wrist and pinned her against the wall. She smirked, reveling in the dangerous game, finally able to let loose now that the girls were away at camp.

Jordana Kagan

Play

"Your right."

She lifted her leg.

"Lead with your right."

She tried again. Spun once. Fell. Stood. Stared somberly at her sister until the girls toppled from the effort of stifling their laughter and began rolling in the clovers.

Joy.

Flirting

"You're so nice. I can see you getting raped."

I giggled.

Why did I giggle?

"I mean, not in a bad way. You know, you're just so nice, you probably wouldn't tell a guy, no."

Grace choked on a scream as hot tears splashed into the soapy water.

"I know how to say no."

She scrubbed harder on the soiled cotton.

"Yeah. I'm just saying. Like, it's a good thing, you know?"

Apprehension.

"A good thing to be raped?"

"No. No. No. A good thing to be nice. Like, you wouldn't be a bitch and reject a guy."

Jordana Kagan

Shattered Dreams

"Fuck me!"

"Please. No."

"*Fuck me!*"

He raged as she tried to fend off his blows, tried in vain to escape.

Violence.

New Reality

"Time. What the heck was that?"

Silence.

"Three seconds off. The meet's this Saturday. College recruiters. Championships. What's goin' on with you?"

"I..." Head hanging, she couldn't continue.

Shame.

Jordana Kagan

April Showers

The wind roars. The rain assaults me—stinging, icy hot
bullets mark my cheeks and chin. Undeterred, I climb past
rock and fog to the top of the cliff. My coat, blown out like a
sail, carries me backward by an invisible force. I refuse to
succumb. Something is here and I must give witness. But
understanding precedes expression, and I have not yet found
words to describe this moment.

The Intern

Grace searched methodically, drowning out the muffled moans from behind the closed door.

"Yes!" Several million views and thousands of comments. She shared the link and heard the phone ping next door.

"Music for constipation?" He pressed play. The sounds of water and binaural beats echoed off the tiles. "Now find me something for the goddamned hemorrhoids!"

"Yes, sir, Mr. President." *The sun never sets on interns at the White House*, she thought amusedly.

No Love Lost

They had broken up before. Off and on for years. This time was different. She was sick, physically nauseous, at the thought.

"Why don't you want to be with me?" She begged to understand. She'd known they were meant for each other from the moment she'd laid eyes on him.

It was carnal at first, but then the friendship developed. Then trust, and comfort. She convinced herself that she had everything he was looking for.

He called that night to break their date and followed it up with, "I don't think we should do this anymore." Grace was stunned. They talked in circles for 45 minutes as she sat in the parking lot and missed her kickboxing class. He wasn't in love with her, he said.

"I don't understand," she said. They kept getting back together *because* they loved each other. They *worked* together.

"I love you, but I'm not in love with you," he tried again.

She couldn't accept that.

"You know that sweet pain you feel?"

Her breath caught in her throat.

"I could never feel that for you."

Hope-less

A bird lands on the bare branch. Weightless, swaying in the breeze. The weather has warmed, but the leaves are cautious, knowing fickle Nature for what she is. To emerge now is a risk. Sun today, yes, but there is no guarantee for tomorrow.

I wish I had been cautious like the leaves. I wish I had not been so easy to trust.

But desperation begets blind hope. And so, she still believes.

Jordana Kagan

Amazing Grace

"You know, I'm almost a hundred now." She sits at the table in her red-and-black striped shirt and lilac apron. Her name, Grace, is embroidered in white thread on the front pocket. Her smile is pure honey and sweetness.

"It's clear to me that someone up there got us mixed up. I'm going to show you this, in color—not living color, mind you, but color."

I take the folded papers of Daniel's obituary. Her printer mustn't be working properly. The colored pictures are blurred and look like 3D images sans glasses. Many colors. Many silhouettes. Nothing aligned.

"A mother should never have to bury her son."

I marvel at this woman with wispy white hair, elongated jowls, and glassy blue eyes; the matriarch who loves to look at the beautiful clouds, the mother who has lost her son.

"Forgive me for saying this," she says, "but I just don't have anything left in me anymore."

I wonder at the circumstances of life.

Henry

Go Figure

"You're right." The teacher smiled.
    "I am?" the child dared.
    "You are."
    The boy beamed.
    Pride.

Jordana Kagan

School Daze

"Time exists in the space of reality..."

"We'll get caught," he mouthed as the lecturer droned on.

"No one will know," she countered.

He licked his lips. Dry. Nerves.

She winked and stood, her notebook spread open on the table.

Seduction.

Choking

"I just... We were just... Oh, my God." Henry couldn't continue. He ran his hand again through his now disheveled hair and paced between the tables.

"Sir, it's okay."

"We..."

The officer motioned for an EMT to bring a blanket. "Sir, I understand this is difficult. Please just take a breath and relax. We just need to know what happened."

"What the fuck!" He said it more to himself than to the others—and there were others. At least a dozen now. Officers, reporters, waiters. *What the fuck!* He was tugging at his hair again.

"Sir?" The officer paused and waited for him to make eye contact. "Sir, we are going to need a statement."

Henry sat down at the table and stared across the plates to where Sabrina had been sitting. "We were just eating. She ordered the chutney platter, and when she was dipping into the mango chutney, I started telling a joke. I got to the punchline as she was chewing the naan and mango chutney. And then...and then...she was laughing. I mean, I thought she was laughing. And then I guess I realized she, I mean, I...I realized she was choking, so I jumped up and tried to help her cough it up, you know? Like I was hitting her on the back to try and help her get it out, and then the waiter came over, and I guess he pushed me out of the way to do the

Heimlich maneuver, and I mean, I guess, I mean…" Henry broke off.

"Sir?"

"It was only our second date. I mean, what the fuck!"

Get Lucky

Henry was everything she wanted in a man.

Attractive.

Athletic.

Intelligent.

Underneath the scruffy hair, the nerdy glasses, and the dusty Merrells was a superhot, super thoughtful, super great guy. Their first date was a walk around the neighborhood. She never trusted guys straight off the app, so as with all first encounters, she suggested they meet at the grocery store. They headed off from there.

He impressed her. His goofy, bashful grin. His insightful ruminations. His passion. She appreciated the fact that he didn't try to kiss her that night. Or the next. They simply enjoyed the experience of getting to know one another as they padded their way up and down the hills of the suburban enclave.

It was the third night out—an actual dinner date—that sealed their fate.

Gourmet pizza.

Fresh basil.

Chocolate brownie á la mode.

And then, the kiss.

The one she had been anticipating, fantasizing about for eleven days. The soft, tingling pressure of his lips against hers. Their mouths parted. Tongues touched. And inside she shriveled because his mouth tasted like the smell of her dental floss after eating gorgonzola and grapes.

Play demure, she told herself as she gently pulled away, smiling coyly.

Snow Days

I've been staring at the snow for more than an hour. It's been falling for longer, but I only woke up an hour ago. It wasn't supposed to snow today, but it looks like it's not going to stop.

It was still dark when I first saw it. White flecks sparkling under the streetlamp. It was like a movie. Picturesque. Now the sky is white. Everything is white. The cars. The sidewalk. My fire escape is holding several inches. The flakes are racing down in huge clumps. It's quiet. No one else is awake, I suppose, but I'm sure if I go out to Stop & Shop, I'll encounter the assholes. The ones who don't know how to drive, the ones who don't pick up after their dogs, the ones who piss against buildings and desecrate the peaceful purity of the city sleeping beneath this white blanket.

Disaster Strikes

"Great idea. Great. Fantastic."

If I didn't know better, I'd believe him.

Looking around the room, Henry realized that the entire team was roped in... *Until Cardozo betrays one of them.*

Henry had always been vigilant, but Cardozo brought down his defenses. Shadows of red flags, flickers of alarm—all dismissed and disarmed. Judging by present company, Henry wasn't the only one Cardozo had neutralized.

"That's exactly the kind of thing we're looking for!" Cardozo said. He had already charmed his next victim.

Circle of Life

"Time." The word garbled through his phlegm.

"It's time," he ventured again, before Life left.

I bent my head closer to grasp the last of his essence.

Transition.

Caleb

Full Bars

Caleb checked his phone. Again. Full bars.

She saw the message. Why isn't she answering? He cursed her, then berated himself for seeming too eager.

That was the problem, they said. He didn't have anything else going on.

The Void.

That was the problem.

Jordana Kagan

Revenge

Their mouths stop moving when they see me. I smell of sex.
The scent is heavy. It suffocates the cigarettes, perfume, and
cologne. It overpowers the weed and the ocean.

I feel vibrations from the bass pounding deep inside. It
keeps rhythm with my pulse. And I keep walking. Counting
each step, 'cause otherwise I'll explode.

There Was a Reason

"Fuck me? Fuck you. Fuck you, you whore."
   Betrayal.

Jordana Kagan

Not Today

Hurry up and wait. Story of my life. I get to a location 'cause someone somewhere decided that something was urgent. So I drop everything and run. And then wait. And wait. 'Cause they don't actually need it *now*, they needed it three days ago, but they didn't tell me until today, and by the time I get here, after sitting in traffic, the goddamn building is closed. Un-fucking-believable.

Be the Change

The Russians had the right idea—people need to start disappearing. We aren't supposed to live like this. We aren't supposed to adapt to this shit.

Some people can. What's that say about them, huh?

And what's it mean for the rest of us who can't?

Jordana Kagan

Mating Season

Mesmerized by the shadows of my potted plants,
Traversing the wall,
Framed in hues of summer sorbet, the colors of sunrise—

Gazing at birds floating and hopping, chirping their cheer,
From the bed of the studio apartment—

I expect the ding of the elevator.
I wait for the jingle of keys.
I brace for the click of the lock.
The fall of footsteps.
The zipper.
You.
Ready to unleash your wrath.

Perspective

Should it matter? Probably not, but it does. 'Cause if my actions don't make a difference, why the hell should I bother doing anything? Why make that investment?

I'm not goin' outta my way for someone who hasn't earned it. If I bend over backwards to accommodate some bitch, or, even worse, if I bend over backwards to try and impress a girl before she's done anything to deserve it, then I've fallen off the tracks.

So, what is important? I'm important. What I'm doing is important. The future I'm making. That's important. What some undeserving whore thinks of me, that's not important. But I've been letting that take over. My mistake. Not to be repeated.

That's a lot of pressure. It means I gotta constantly think about what I'm doing and why. I need to remember—'cause if it doesn't add up, I gotta get out.

Jordana Kagan

Alternate Endings

"You're right."
   "I see."
   "I would have told you."
   "Yeah. It's not important."
   "I would have told you eventually."
   "It doesn't matter now."
   Resentment.

Reflection

I hear her wailing from the window. I can't make out the words, but I feel her pain. I feel his rage. I would call for help, but I can't identify the source of the screams. By the time the cops arrive, he'll be done with her. I know this from experience. There is no escape.

When it's over, I peer at the window. I see our reflections in the glass. Me. A trembling, tangled mess of hair. A bloody nose. Red welts that will turn deep purple. Him. A man turning away. His fury spent.

Jess

An Even Exchange

The humiliation of reality, one escaped prison exchanged for another. He is from the Eastern Bloc, was no doubt promised a better life abroad.

But now abroad, he cleans filth and sewage. He is ignored and forgotten as he makes his way among the people who are too busy and too important to see him.

Jordana Kagan

Championships

The presentation hall was filled to capacity with parents and their smallest children. The older ones were all seated on stage, on display. Jess was participating in the final round, though she didn't know it. The blocking device prevented her from hearing and seeing the progress she and the others were making.

She used the silence to review the rules in her mind until her thoughts were interrupted by the moderator.

"For the championship, what is seventy-five percent expressed as a fraction?"

The championship? I made it? Seventy-five percent expressed as a fraction was easy. *Too easy*, Jess thought. She wondered if it was a trick but didn't have time to dillydally.

"Seventy-five percent expressed as a fraction is seventy-five over a hundred, which can be reduced to three over four," she said warily.

"Congratulations." The moderator's dry voice sounded in the earpiece.

Jess was now a Primary.

Level Up, Hot Stuff

He was cute, but like most guys these days, he had Bitch Body—narrow shoulders, soft hips, undefined arms, and a round tummy. His hairline was still intact, so Jess assumed he was a Primary like her.

"You look a lot older than fifteen," he said.

An unspecified warning flashed across her prefrontal cortex.

Jess scrutinized his face in the dim light. Wrinkles, subtle etchings of crow's-feet, puppet mouth…and dry hands, which meant he had been outside—*like a Worker would be*. There was a shadow of hair curling up from his collar. *Primaries don't have hair there, not unless they're Athletes and shooting T*. Jess smiled instinctively at the thought.

Bitch Bod misread it as an invitation and leaned in. Jess took one measured step back.

She was on track, scheduled to make Levels at eighteen. She still had three years to go, but she was in good standing and wasn't about to mess it up on some half-brain Worker who was creeping at a party for Primaries. The government had actually scoped her. They needed robust young minds like hers. They needed people who could do long division. *I'm amazing at long division*, Jess thought as she turned on her heels and walked toward the subterranean transport.

Bitch Bod, rejected and twitching in anger, had no cards left to play.

Jordana Kagan

Waiting Room

"Time?"

    "3:37."

    "What's taking so long? What's a matter, d'you think?"

    "I don't know, hon. I don't know."

    Fear.

Streaming Live

"Why isn't anyone stopping them? Someone needs to do something." Jess was frightened.

"What do you want them to do? It's not their fight."

"But they know it's wrong. Someone should do something." *It wasn't supposed to be like this*, Jess thought.

Their voices continued in this way as a boy on-screen was beaten to a mutilated pulp. Keepers were able to apprehend the assailant, a seventeen-year-old from the same Level as the boy who was now lying in a coma—who was only fourteen. No one truly understands what caused the incident; the livestream didn't start until the first punch had been thrown. Thank God for little miracles like livestream. Without it, we would be eating each other alive.

Jordana Kagan

Decipher

The sky is blue today. Maybe tomorrow they'll let us go outside.

They showed us a movie yesterday. It made Patricia cry, so they turned it off.

They changed the night routine. We can't close our doors. The hall lights are bright. No one sleeps anymore.

Patricia killed herself. I haven't gone outside yet.

Dex wants to escape. I don't see how. They are always watching. What do they want from us?

It's like living in a petri dish. I wish they would just tell us what to do so we could get out of here. Dex says we're the only ones left. He says they killed all the others. He says the black clouds are smoke from all the burning bodies. I think he's right.

They moved us all into one big room. There's no privacy. Do you think Jase is still out there? I miss having a brother.

Dex is gone.

They tried to tell me something. I couldn't understand them. They didn't use words. They wanted to show me. I wasn't scared. I saw. But I didn't understand.

Jordana Kagan

Slim Pickings

The polish was chipping. Thin cracks webbed across the Luscious Lavender lacquer that had been sitting too long on the shelf but not long enough on her nails. Once immaculate, the nails were now jagged and frayed.

She continued to pick at the polish, which mangled another layer of nail bed. She ripped and bit the cuticles. She didn't care if they noticed. *Let them see*, she thought in defiance.

Thrice screwed by the circumstances: first, the Ascent; then, the Selection; finally, the Purging. She watched in guilt-torn horror as three-quarters of the world burned. But not her. Jess was special. *Fucking long division!*

She wanted to bleed. If she could render her hands useless, they would have to release her. So she reasoned. Sadly, that miscalculation would lead to a fourth screwing. But Jess didn't know that yet.

Heavy Metal

Metal grinding against the rails. Extended misery seeping into my thoughts—

No.

I resist. Pluck the images of torture from my mind.

It's the unknown that frightens me. That terror grips me more firmly than the unyielding confines of this box. This prison. This uniform.

This reality they created only half resembles life— mockery enough that people remain sedated and subdued, quietly following one another like ants, neatly arranged and easily crushed.

This is what my parents saw. This is what I see now. Whether escape is possible, I do not yet know.

Anonymous

The Outsider

I know I am here.
The biting wind tells me so,
As it slices through exposed skin.

They don't see,
As I kneel
On my soggy piece of cardboard.

They are on their way to
Work
School
The store

To buy food,
To find warmth,
To escape...me.

Some say the world will end in fire.
I know it ends in ice.
Frozen out of this life,
I kneel
On a tattered pulp of cardboard
That cannot bear my weight.

Jordana Kagan

Rituals

"Be open, but don't force it. If you force it, you'll forget."

"Maybe I want to forget."

"Hush. Don't say that." Oma gently rebuked her granddaughter. This was a sacred ritual. The old woman, a guide for the younger.

The girl raged inside. The big people were incessantly instructing her in what to say and think and do, always making her feel insignificant. She was the one with the power, with the pen. Yet she was forced to smother her words in order to maintain the peace. That was the price.

She pressed her lips together and harnessed the rebuttal. Then she grasped the pen that would allow her to finally express the fullness of her inner world.

Common Humanity

She is a heavy-set woman pushing a cleaning cart. She stops beside the bathroom entrance, aware of all the restless people rushing to make their flights. They register the nuisance of this bulky frame blocking their path but are otherwise unaware of her.

She has red-rimmed ice-blue eyes. Brown waves frame her bloated, lined face. I smile but she doesn't see. She stares beyond me with a look that translates her invisibility.

"Good morning," I say.

She warms for one moment, mirrors my expression.

Then she reenters her world of the unseen.

Jordana Kagan

Two Hearts

Two hearts took turns beating—
Alternating.
Because it was too painful—
Otherwise.
The souls attached to them agreed—
United.
They could not endure much longer.

Convulsions

Violent, rhythmic convulsions propel him—
Thrusting back and forth,
Forcing him side to side.
What malady is this? I wonder.

He is like me,
Blanketed in gray filth and grime.
From him wafts the sticky odor of fear
And sweat
And solitary nights:
The smell of decay.
Swollen ankles and gout betray his poverty and pain.

Whereas I am invisible, his state compels him into their sight,
So that they must employ deliberate ignorance,
Effortful avoidance.
They consciously stay away.
Of me, they take no note.
I do not offend their senses and sensibilities.
Today.
By comparison.
It's all relative.

Jordana Kagan

Winter

I am sitting on the frigid bench. It's covered in graffiti. The splintered wood cuts through the temperature technology of my heaviest coat, and the backs of my legs are numb. My feet, swaddled in rubber, faux fur, and wool socks, don't stand a chance against the concrete. Maybe because I'm not standing—haha, get it?

In times like these, one must maintain one's cheer.

Phenomenon

"That's strange," I say to no one in particular.

I lift my eyes and scan the room. There are at least three people who could have heard me. It's reasonable to suppose they did, but I'm effectively invisible. To them, my dangling remark could have been a fly buzzing. I spent many years talking to myself as if I were alone. Others treated me accordingly, ignored me. And now? Now, I am in the habit of speaking my mind to no one in particular.

Occasionally, I'll receive a "What's that?" from the uninitiated. A "Pardon me?" from those who know no better. The best course of action, I have learned, is for *me* to ignore *them*. I fortify myself against those kind, well-intentioned intrusions, repeating my affirmations and forgiving them— for they know not what they do.

"Very strange," I continue. Because what I just saw *is* strange. But I have no person with whom to corroborate.

If I had taken after my mother, the prattle would never cease. She speaks aloud to no one in particular, as if everyone in her vicinity is waiting for her to speak. My observations indicate that this is the case: They are waiting for her to speak—just so they may respond. It's very bizarre, but not as bizarre as—I'm sure my eyes were playing a trick on me.

Jordana Kagan

Just Deserts

"Fuck me."

He realized his mistake.

"Fuck me."

The irreparable harm he'd caused.

"Fuck me."

His fingers interlaced with the trigger.

Repentance.

Creatures

Enamel

Thank you for coming to hear my story. The circumstances are bizarre, I admit. I know you're wondering how I came to be like this. It all started with a clogged drain.

It was November when I noticed my shower was backed up. It didn't seem serious; water still went down—slowly. I ignored the problem for as long as I could—that is to say, until two weeks later when, midway through my shower, I found myself standing in a tub half-full of soapy, dirty water. I was forced to act. Drano, snakes, plungers. I fixed it, no problem. For good measure, I bought a hair catcher to ensure the drain wouldn't clog again.

That purchase rattled my sense of reality. I knew my hair had been thinning—no one could deny it—but most forty-year-olds deal with this dilemma. I hadn't been concerned until the hair catcher confronted me with the truth. This was beyond regular hair loss.

From then on, I would harvest fistfuls of hair each time I ran my fingers through my once enviable locks. The bald patches were impossible to hide—mottled, hairless islands in a sea of thin wisps. I was too shocked to be embarrassed, and anyway, I was distracted.

You see, around the same time, my skin was feeling very dry and very tight. I bought a vat of moisturizer and all but dunked myself in it twice a day, to no avail. My epidermis was getting worse; it felt rough, like alligator scutes. Then it simply fell off, leaving red rawness beneath.

My nails also started to peel and disintegrate. It was too late by the time I sat down on that fateful day to "scratch" my head. My nails were paper thin by that point, but they still provided some relief when I used them to rub my ailing outer layer. Not realizing the cuticles were also weak, I scratched. And the nails, what was left of them, popped off. The cuticles couldn't hold on to those last vestiges of keratin—that's what it was, as it turned out. My body stopped producing keratin. And collagen. Eventually, I wouldn't be able to create any protein, but I didn't know this at the time.

I sat with bloodied hands, shredded nails, angry scales of red flesh for skin, and broadening bald patches, wondering what was happening.

Then *it* began. My body started aching. From the inside. The joints. The bones. It was terrible. It only took a few more weeks for my body to fully decompose. Without protein, we can't survive, you know. So, I bid farewell to my earthly frame and now I exist in this jar, you see? Just two rows of teeth, talking your ear off. Oh, dear—I didn't mean it like that. Of course, you are a lone ear. How ever did that happen?

So Lonely

"Mwahahahaha."

    . . .

    "Mwahahahaha!"

    . . .

    "Mwahaha-hallo?"

    . . .

"Where did everybody go?" Little Ghost, now timorous, wondered aloud.

Hovering through hallways, Little Ghost continued...in search of others.

Jordana Kagan

Take an Inch

Two mites were positioned side by side staring at the unwelcome guest.

"Yeah. Well, *that's* your problem, right there." Brutus was the bigger of the two, and four *whole* weeks older. He knew things Dmitry didn't.

"What *is* it?" the younger asked.

"It's a root."

"A what?"

"A *root*," Brutus stated.

It was obvious, but not to Dmitry. He was inexperienced in the ways of the world. And he had certainly not been expecting this strange, firm, greenish tube-thing to penetrate his reading nook and crush his favorite rocking chair. Indeed, the small mite had never even *heard* of such a thing happening. Such was the result of soil schooling—so much left out of the curriculum that nymphs didn't even learn the basics anymore.

"A lute?" Dmitry ventured, bashful at his own ignorance.

"A R-O-O-T," Brutus corrected him.

"Oh. A root."

That seemed to solve the matter. The two stared at the firmly planted root that split the cavernous chamber in two.

"What's a root?" the smaller one asked, finally.

At last, Brutus knew what he was put in the earth to do.

A Conversation

"Where were you?"

"I told you I'd be late."

"Where were you?"

"Don't make a big deal out of this."

"Where were you?!"

"Honey."

"Stop evading."

"I'm not."

"Don't lie to me."

"I'm not. Honey. I was with Honey."

"Honey? But I thought... You told me Milk, Chocolate. Honey?"

"I know. Last-minute change. It's something the company is trying out with a new focus group. They've already marketed chocolate milk; now they're trying honeyed chocolate... Don't look so down, Peppermint. We'll have our chance soon."

Jordana Kagan

Moving Day

BEATRICE: As you can see, the foyer is being completely reassembled.

NOELLE: Will these bodies be gone by the time we move in? I'm trying to watch my figure, and the smell of decay simply demands that I gorge.

BEATRICE: Oh, yes. The current feeders are ferociously ravenous. They're transitioning, after all. I shouldn't think anything will be left by solstice.

NOELLE: Oh, good. That's plenty of time, isn't it, Darling?

TERRENCE: It is. Yes. I think it is. Do you know whether the Lord will allow for pets?

BEATRICE: The contract states a maximum of three creatures, but no more than one human. Occasionally, you can get away with two of the big ones—if they're quiet. But you didn't hear it from me.

TERRENCE: We only have a big one.

NOELLE: The little ones make so much noise, don't they?

TERRENCE: They do. They do even after a feeding. But they're sweeter.

BEATRICE: Mmm. That's the trade-off, I suppose. If you'll follow me this way, I'll lead you through the webs down to the tombs...

Rat Man

I watch 'em from my hidin' place and listen.

"We'll start at the top."

They file pas' me one by one.

"And we'll see what we got."

Men in bright orange vests dec'rated with reflective stripes.

"You want me to stay at the platform?"

They all carry somethin'. Bulky toolboxes. Equipment. Dangerous.

"Nah, better come see first."

I'm invisible. Good thing. Don't need 'em calling the Rat Man again. That guy killed the entire den from here to Jamaica. Can't say I'm sen'imental about it, even though half my family and Maud were exterminated. It was disorientin', for sure. I ran up to Queens Bouleva'd to check out the new pizza place, see if there were any scraps. I've been eatin' pretty good since the pandemic, tons of leftovers. Jus' gotta be careful not to let 'em see you. Once they see you, that's it. Kaput. Usually, they don't come down to the subway. And it was so nice out, I figured it couldn't do no harm stayin' out and roamin' about. Neighborhood's changin', that's for sure. I passed by that new park an—I'm doin' it again, huh? I digress. Point is, by the time I get back to Union Turnpike, the whole family is writhin'. Lyin' there squirmin' under the tracks. Nothin' I could do. I watched 'em for a little bit, but how long can ya stand around for that? I figured he left the poison food out again. Supposed to be illegal, but hey, whaddaya gonna do?

Dead Ants

"It's very simple, really. Just keep your mouth shut."

"But—"

"No. Don't be *that* guy."

"But—"

"Mark, we have a procedure. You can't just come in here and overhaul the system when—"

"But—"

"No! Christ. Mark, you're great. You're the best. We get it. That's why we brought you on. Because you're the best."

"I was—"

"Whatever you think, whatever ideas you have, keep them to yourself. We don't need your ideas. We need you to execute."

"You want me to execute bad ideas?"

"We want you to adhere to protocol and procedure."

"Protocol and procedure will get the entire west wing killed."

"Mark, just keep your mouth shut."

Mark thought about the queen and all the workers who were hauling grit, grain by grain, to accommodate the new eggs about to hatch, thousands of larvae—potentially. *If this construction project goes through, none of them will survive. This is deliberate. This is mutiny.*

There was only one thing for Mark to do.

Jordana Kagan

Soiled Again

MANNI: Nah, Willie, I'm telling you. It's way better down
　　here.

WILLIE: That's 'cause you don't know any different. You
　　never been exposed to the big, wide world.

MANNI: You're young; you don't understand.

WILLIE: Oh, I understand plenty. I understand you're trying
　　to hold me back from my dreams.

MANNI: You think you're gonna have all these adventures.
　　Trust me. Stay down here.

WILLIE: Down here is a prison.

MANNI: Down here, you got cover. You know the terrain.
　　It's nice and dark. You're safe here. What we got scares
　　them. They get claustrophobic. They get nervous.

WILLIE: Manni, I get claustrophobic. I get nervous.

MANNI: Listen! Down here they don't know what threats
　　are lurking. Can't see, can't breathe. You and me?
　　We're good here. We're *good*.

WILLIE: I'm not, Manni. I'm not good. I gotta go topsoil. I
　　need to breathe.

MANNI: You're talking suicide, Willie.

WILLIE: I'm talking freedom.

MANNI: Yeah? Okay. Just remember what they say: "The
　　early bird gets the worm."

WILLIE: Wait. Wait... Is *that* what happened to Clyde?

Disenchanted Meadow

Gemma was concerned. Lachlan had not come out to play all afternoon. She missed her friend and wanted to help, but Lachlan wasn't ready to share.

"Sometimes unicorns need to be by themselves," her mother had said. Gemma couldn't understand since she had been a butterfly all her life, but she hoped Lachlan would remember that he wanted to race in the meadow with Jakub and Thomaz, Rosalinde and Gregory. They were planning a special trip, and whoever won the race would get to choose where to go. Everyone knew Lachlan was going to win; he was the fastest and the strongest. He was also the nicest and the funniest, but right now Lachlan was troubled. Gemma perched on his ear, hoping he would say something. Alas, the despondent unicorn could barely lift his head.

"Gemma," he whispered, "I hurt Gregory."

"Oh, no!" Gemma cried as she fluttered to make eye contact.

"Please, don't make me feel worse." Lachlan seemed to sink even more deeply into the grass.

"Oh, Lachlan. I didn't mean to. What happened? It can't be *that* bad. I'm sure he knows it was an accident." Gemma's form floated higher, then dipped gracefully, landing next to Lachlan's left nostril.

The unicorn huffed, throwing Gemma off balance. He rolled onto his side and melted into the ground, slowly extending his right foreleg. That's when Gemma saw the remnants of Gregory and his lustrous shell, dried and caked onto the underside of Lachlan's hoof.

"Oh! Oh, no. Gregory? Lachlan! Gregory! Oh, no!"

Another perilous friendship between fantastical unicorn and terrestrial gastropod ended in sorrow.

Dog-Eat-Dog World

Ensconced in the eternity of dreams
Of rich fields and ripe orchards,
She galloped carefree against the wind,
Into a summer's eve,
Nipping at fireflies,
Smelling the stars.
She panted—
Tongue long, eyes twinkling.

Wrapped in the black velvet of sleep,
She forgot hunger and pain,
Cold and mange.
Harsh words, cruel kicks—
An existence she never chose.

Her paws worked fiercely to keep pace with the visions of
    peace.

Jordana Kagan

Immersive Reading

I was deep in what Michael Csikszentmihalyi has termed *flow*.
That is to say, I was completely immersed and had lost sense
of place and time. Katerina had left me earlier—gone to
locate a book for poolside amusement—allowing me to
peruse the stacks on my own. As I am wont to do, I
meandered into the reference section and took up where I
had previously left off, reading about gastropods in the *World
Book Encyclopedia*. Riveting, really. So much so that I was, as
mentioned, in flow.

This, of course, is why I did not notice when the room
fell silent. It was only when I paused to turn the page that I
broke concentration and noted something awry. Personal
history—and *National Geographic* programs—have taught me
to proceed with caution when things become unnaturally
still. So I took stock.

I was biting the nail of my big toe. It's a peculiar habit I
exhibit when reading fascinating expository texts. I
suspended all gnashing and sucking and slowly removed the
moist digit from my mouth. I had collected a small but
interested audience during my brief encounter with snails on
page 197.

Katerina, sensing a threat to her offspring and always
eager to demonstrate her maternal prowess, scooped me up
with one hand and gathered my left shoe and sock with the
other (how she also managed to also abscond with her

Danielle Steel novel, I will never know) and thus briskly exited the haven that is the library to deposit me firmly into my car seat. I promptly began to cry. Oh, how I long to be a thirty-six-month-old in the fiftieth percentile. Would that I could. Would that I could!

Jordana Kagan

Redwoods

I stare through the latticed branches at the azure sky. The Redwoods are my protectors. Finally, I rest.

I wake to a chill, my back moist from the damp earth. There was a noise, a—something indistinct. I turn to see the silken web. Beyond the gossamer, something red. I focus. A maple leaf. A flicker of understanding before my mind is swallowed by the dark abyss.

My eyes open, but I have yet to look. For fear. They are already here. The sound of their jaws employed, a death knell. I feel them inside me.

I am the Maple: worn from mountains, dusty from deserts, eager to be planted anew. I am the Maple carrying a pestilence. I feel the weight of the Loopers canvassing my trunk, the multiplying mass now invading my protectors. There is no redemption for a betrayal such as this. In the arms of the Redwoods, I shall die. I beg your mercy, Preservers of Life, for you will join me. Together we return to Mother Earth. Together, a forsaken forest.

Dosin

Prologue

There was no shortage of bodies on Dosin. That's why the Levators came, to harvest the bodies. There had been rebellion initially. Minds unwilling to be sacrificed. Occasionally, souls still fought to escape the corporeal prison by killing the flesh so they could be free. The Levators had a remedy for this, naturally. They needed the bodies.

Stay

"A broken heart is a repentant heart. You must repent."

"Repent? For what?"

The hushed audience stared incredulously at the young interloper. After "redeeming" her parents, the leaders reluctantly tolerated the notion that she could be won over, but they were not convinced. She had been a thorn in their side and now, this. This generous opportunity for Univer to repent was the last step before the compelled "redemption." She would transition the same way her parents had.

The audience hummed like a swarm of wasps, anticipating and lethal. A wave of contempt swelled through their cocked eyebrows and vitriolic stares.

The Speaker was immensely satisfied that the girl had confirmed his suspicions. "Ms. Univer, I do not approve your conditional stay. I am loath to accept you as one of Us. You know of my antipathy toward your family, for they were traitors."

Univer, still standing, protested. "I have nothing for which to repent." She was defiant and bitter. She was, in fact, still in turmoil. The cult had taken her youth, but she was not aware of it, not until her birth mother and birth father began to reeducate her. She had not fully understood how or where they lived prior to Dosin, only that suddenly there was an enemy and she, Univer, must desperately internalize the strange lessons her parents were determined to instill.

They implanted a new truth. She promised to water it until the time was right. She hadn't known the consequences. She understood now, four years later—four years orphaned—what was at stake. She held firm.

Jordana Kagan

No Escape

My throat wraps around the spicy liquid,
An effort to stop its descent.
While peristaltic waves commence without consent.
Muscles release and contract.
My body betrays me again.

It's blindingly bright even through closed lids.
This means one thing: I have returned.

I took the step to kill myself.
My body rejected the gesture.
They took a step to kill my soul.
My body embraced the "Savior."
Traitor!

They are watching.
I see the monitors; they see me.

Time is inadequate.
This is why I fight.
This is why I fight to die.
This is why they force me alive.

Waiting

Again. Always again.

She stared past her hands on the steering wheel, through the windshield, beyond the combines, at the blazing lights. She hated herself. Loathed her inability to, just once, say "No." To, just once, not give in. But the torment in her head—it was all in her mind. *Wasn't it?* That's what they had told her. The Levators. With their advanced technology and intergalactic experience, they were the caste entrusted with the safety of Dosin. It seemed as if she was the only one who wasn't safe.

Jordana Kagan

Running

My arm is bleeding; I removed the Piru, but I have it. I
brought it with me. They taught me that the Levators can't
track me when it's outside the body. There are other ways to
track, but the Piru can't measure my vitals if it's not in me. It
can't sense me breathing. It can't be certain I'm not dead.

Dogs. The dogs can track the smell, but I'm wearing an
Odus uniform. That will block my blood smell.

Tristan. They can torture him. He won't tell. Not to save
himself. But if he thinks he can save me... It will be my fault.
I have to hurry.

Last Stand

No! Shit. "Sir, enemy advancing. Troops and armor in the open!"

"Range?"

"Seven hundred meters and closing."

The dogs snarled.

The radio crackled.

Tragedy.

Jordana Kagan

Impasse

She sat in front of them for what felt like days. It was likely only mere minutes. She had no way of knowing—the brightly lit room masked all indicators of time.

They gave her a choice.

How to proceed?

One path was sure death. The other, unimaginable anguish. Both selfish. But she had to choose.

"We will make it worthwhile," the faceless voices articulated.

They were all faceless ethereal beings. For them, the choice was clear.

If They Could See Me Now

"This doesn't make sense." I rub my eyes. Blink. Take off my glasses. Rub again.

"I can see." Without the thick corrective lenses. For the first time since—for the first time I can remember. "I can see."

I squeeze the red indentation, angry from years of carrying the weight on the bridge of my nose. I was only two when it happened. At least, that's what they told me.

But—

They also told me I'd never be able to see again. Without the lenses. Maybe I'm dreaming. This could be a dream.

But—

They monitor dreams. Subconscious thoughts are dangerous. At least, that's what they told me.

But—

If this isn't a dream...

Jordana Kagan

Epilogue

In the beginning,
God created the heavens and the earth.
In the end, it didn't matter.

In the beginning,
Man claimed his place as king among beasts.
In the end, he fought himself extinct.

In the beginning,
We sallied forth—a desperate mission, a hopeless venture.
In the end, we conquered that foolish God and his man-made
    jesters.

And now, we create
A new beginning.

Index

Acknowledgements

Ben and Seth. My brothers. My sanity. I love you. *Mom*. You have chiseled me into the imperfect masterpiece that I am. *Liz*. You insisted I pursue. *Reb*. Thank you for your unwavering support. *Brigante. José. Jamie*. The Alpha Males-cum-Beta Readers. Thank you for your encouragement on this project. *Students*. You are my teachers and my inspirations. Thank you for reminding me why life is. *Paul*. You challenge me to be better. Every day.

About the Author

Jordana Kagan is a teacher, trainer, writer, and performer. She maintains the website beatsbooksbarbells.com. This is her first book.

www.ingramcontent.com/pod-product-compliance
Lightning Source LLC
Chambersburg PA
CBHW020636250626
47154CB00008B/2703